ONE MONDAY MORNING

ONE MONDAY MORNING

by Uri Shulevitz

A Sunburst Book / Farrar Straus Giroux

One Monday Morning is an elaboration of the ancient French folk song
"Lundi matin, l'emp'reur, sa femme . . ."

Distributed in Canada by Douglas & McIntyre Ltd.
Printed and bound in China
First published by Charles Scribner's Sons, 1967
First Sunburst edition, 2003
1 3 5 7 9 10 8 6 4 2

Library of Congress Cataloging-in-Publication Data
Shulevitz, Uri, 1935–
    One Monday morning / by Uri Shulevitz.— 1st Sunburst ed.
        p.   cm.
    "A Sunburst book."
    Summary: In this elaboration on an ancient French song, a king, queen, and
prince with an increasingly large retinue try to pay a call on a young boy who is
rarely home.
    ISBN 0-374-45648-8 (pbk.)
    [1. City and town life—Fiction.   2. Kings, queens, rulers, etc.—Fiction.]
I. Title.

PZ7.S5594 On 2003
[E]—dc21
                                                            2002028809

To Ehud

One Monday morning

the king,

the queen, and the little prince came to visit me.

But I wasn't home.

So the little prince said,
"In that case we shall return on Tuesday."

On Tuesday morning the king, the queen, the little prince,

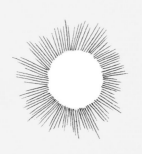

and the knight came to visit me.

But I wasn't home.

So the little prince said,
"In that case we shall return on Wednesday."

On Wednesday morning
the king,
the queen,
the little prince,
the knight,
and the royal guard
came to visit me.

But I wasn't home.

So the little prince said,
"In that case we shall return on Thursday."

On Thursday morning
the king, the queen,
the little prince,
the knight, the royal guard,
and the royal cook
came to visit me.

But I wasn't home.

So the little prince said,
"In that case we shall return on Friday."

On Friday morning
the king, the queen,
the little prince,
the knight, the royal guard,
the royal cook,
and the royal barber
came to visit me.

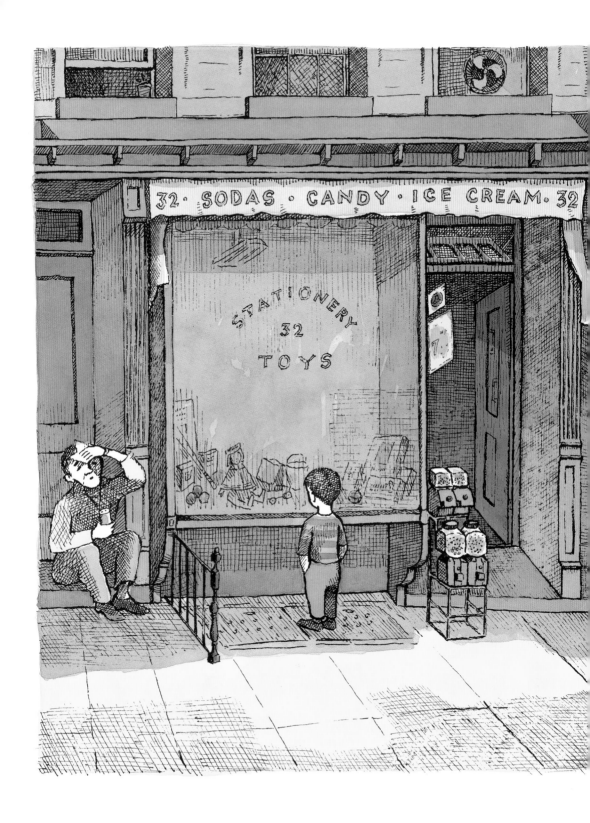

But I wasn't home.

So the little prince said,
"In that case we shall return on Saturday."

On Saturday morning
the king, the queen,
the little prince,
the knight, the royal guard,
the royal cook,
the royal barber,
and the royal jester
came to visit me.

But I wasn't home.

So the little prince said,
"In that case we shall return on Sunday."

On Sunday morning the king, the queen, the little prince, the knight, the royal guard,

the royal cook,
the royal barber,
the royal jester,
and a little dog
came to visit me.

And I was home.
So the little prince said,
"We just dropped in to say hello."